MATHEMATICS OF LIFE AND LOVE

By

Diana D. Deocareza

ACKNOWLEDGEMENT

The author wishes to express her sincerest gratitude to the following persons who contributed and extended their valuable assistance in the preparation and completion of this book.

Dr. Cherrylou D. Repia, CESO V, Schools Division Superintendent, for helping the author in order to make the book a well-done achievement;

Dr. ROSEMARIE C. BLANDO, OIC-Chief, Education Program Supervisor, for helping the author for the improvement of the book;

Mr. FERDINAND E. PASCUAL, Chief SGOD, for the worthy comments and suggestions which have been most helpful in the improvement of the book;

GOV. REBECCA "NINI" YNARES, for her convincingly conveyed a spirit of kindness and generosity for funding the "Iskolar ni Gob for Teachers" program where the author is among the recipients that take part in the completion of this book;

Mrs. EDNA Q. RAMOS, District Supervisor of Rodriguez, Rizal, her best friend, who always motivated the author;

Dr. MARIBETH R. DE DIOS, formerly District Supervisor, for the professional assistance that

greatly contributed to the refinement of the book;

Mrs. MINERVA C, DAVID, District Supervisor of Angono, for her genuine support provided to the author.

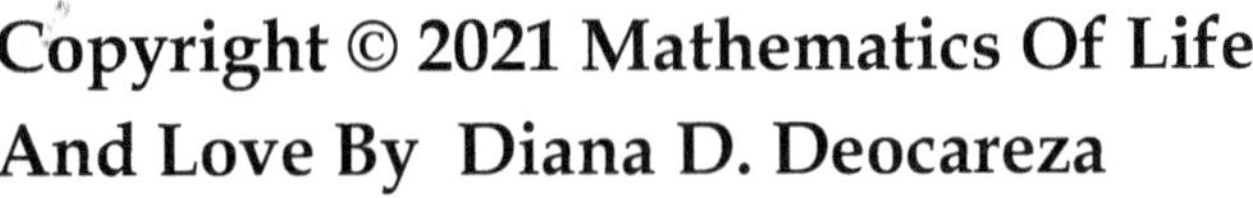

Copyright © 2021 Mathematics Of Life And Love By Diana D. Deocareza

ISBN:
978-621-8253-77-3 - Softbound
978-621-8253-78-0 - Hardbound
978-621-8253-79-7 - Mobile/Kindle

Published by Poetry Planet Book Publishing House
Edited by Marie Ezekiel
Designed by Tess Ritumalta
Photos by Diana D. Deocareza

Some photos used are taken in penterest and may contain its own copyrights

PREFACE

The verses and rhymes inscribed in this book contains meaningful life experiences mirroring the deepest thoughts and emotions of the Author.

Life is Math, metaphorically speaking, throughout our entire lifetime, counting, calculating and solving, the happiness we experience, the sadness that passes us by, the challenges we face and even the people we love, we adore, and even those we never really knew.

Diana, a mathematics Teacher experimented on expressing her thoughts and feelings other than math through poetry…yet discovered that in our journey to life, Math always coexist. Her book contained expressions combining and summing up the value of love, sadness and joy.

Her overflowing meditations, that she scribbled in ink resulted in the creation of her very own book.

Indeed, the author not only bask in beauty, intellect, determination and love…but has challenged herself to enter more doors of opportunity and writing through poetry.

As you open her book, open another Ma'am Diana in a world no one ever thought she can build…

The Publisher

TABLE OF CONTENTS

ADDITION OF "YOU"

I'm maybe the most beautiful
But if I don't have "you",
what is beauty after all…

I may have the fairest skin
If "you" cannot feel its softness
Then I remain worthless..

I may have the most gracious smile
But where are the twinkles in my eyes
If "you" are not here by my side…

What is a rose that blossoms in winter
Only to be frozen by the weather
For only "you" can make it warmer…

You may add one to a zero
But the answer is only "you"
To make life even, it takes two…

My world will complete its addition
If I have love to share all my blessings
To sum "you" brings total happiness…

SUBTRACTION AND LOVE

What is a rainbow?
When yellow is gone
What awaits a sunflower,
If not illuminated by the sun…

What happens to birds,
 If they can't land on trees
What begets the mornings,
Without the sunrise to peep..

Vanity are my lips
when giggles are muted
What causes to merry
if loneliness has spoken…

The melody of my soul slowly fades
If dying alone becomes an ill-fate…

The moment you disappeared
You subtracted LOVE
In my dimming world….

MULTIPLICATION OF YOUR LOVE

The crickets sing in midnight melody
The moon smiles appreciating serenity
My heart hears only wonderful symphony
As your love multiples, it rejoices quietly…

In my garden blossoms beautiful flowers
It used to be barren now filled with colors
You watered it with love and affections
It grows with bursting attractions…

You took me to the top of the world
A star that shines among the luminaries
I am in cloud-nine dancing like an angel
Your love became my wings to fly higher!

Who needs fame and wealth
If I have you to be contend with
You are the multiplication to all that I'm lack
You are a rare gem I will carry in my heart!

DIVISION OF FEELINGS

Cold sweats,
Trembling knees
Heart beats in race
Melt like ice cream
Under this heat..

Unexplained feelings
Upon your nearness
Felt like disappearing
But something within
Leaps with rejoicing!

Oh! But the scary moments
For unrequited emotions
Dividing the excitements
Into the doubt of "what if's".

The tango of life
Of forwards and backwards
Too coward to try
The dance of love…

The divided feelings
Of loving….

FRACTION OF LIFE

Tiny things in life
Has beauty to share
They occupy small parts
But necessary in every way..

You may feel negligible
For things you cannot do
But try to discover
Your gift hidden!

God made us uniquely
With qualities differently
Others may not see it
But everyone has a segment!..

The fraction of life
Divided in diverse part
But cannot create a whole
Without each other's contribution…

Y AND X

Redefine my feelings
Using your arithmetic
Calculate my heart beats
And give me answers
Why it aches and in joy it leaps!

The Y of love is infinite
The X of pain is absolute
Give me the solution
Of Y plus X in a relationship!

Does it hurt much?
When X is greater than Y
When the plus factor
Is not enough to make it even…

So tell me dear
With a square root of two
Altnough there's X in you,
Y will overshadow…

YOU MULTIPLY ME

In the addition to life,
I found the one.
Though I divide it all,
I stood still and tall.

My time seems less,
For myself, I left nothing.
Give it all that's how it is,
Loving you, giving my best.

As time passes by,
You subtract me by and by.
I was broken then,
But somehow I've learned.

Through God, I multiply,
Blossomed and flew high.
Now, I soar with pride,
Moving on as my past had died.

MATH WORKS

Let us Count
one lover for a love
one kiss to be whole
one heart for all
one is precious indeed

two people becomes one
two to tango they say
two hearts can bind
two-gether we stand

three words for I love you
three for I miss you
three for I hate you
three choices to crush or upbuild.

Four seasons to weather
four moods to traverse
four moments to cycle
four we enjoy, pass by, let go or fear

Five for high five
five fingers five toes
five works well together
five makes work well-done.

six might mean imperfection
six six six many fear

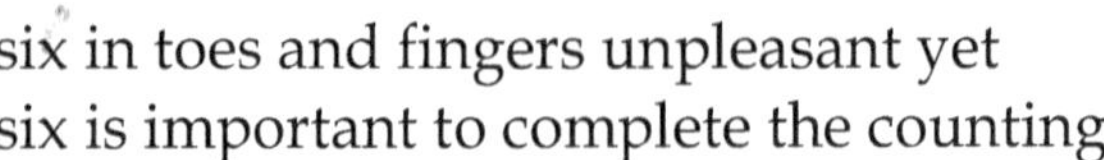

six in toes and fingers unpleasant yet
six is important to complete the counting

seven means forever
seven times to forgive
seven leads to hope
seven happiness awaits

eight glasses of water
eight hours of sleep
eight hours for work
eight completes our day

nine ten eleven
more numbers to count
add or even
look around math works!

SIXTEEN

One, is for me.
Two, becomes we.
Three, roses are not gray.
Four, promises I recall.

Five, I thank God I'm alive.
Six, you became weak.
Seven, you found new heaven.
Eight, I cried with hate.

Nine, months I thought was mine.
Ten, somehow you pretend.
Eleven, you said you were leaving.
Twelve, are the days I grieve.

Thirteen, life shines again.
Fourteen, so, I let it end.
Fifteen, that's my age then.
Sixteen, too young not to learn.

MAYBE ONE DAY

Maybe one day,
I will be free to soar higher
than the tree.
Like eagles, you'll see.

Maybe one day.
I could speak louder and say,
No men shall be slaves and
Love springs in the month of May.

Maybe one day,
Children will know the value
And the worth of humility.
God-fearing and family.

Maybe one day,
Maybe it's today.
Maybe if you only,
Maybe you'll see.

EQUATION

Upon the four corners,
Moving world and wonders.
A weighing of numbers,
And premonition of words.

There's a balance,
A way of goodness and evil.
An equation of choices,
To live in darkness or light.

Destiny and plans,
A kairos in our hands.
Our understanding and demands,
For good life and romance.

This equation and equilibrium,
Is a perfect creation of the One.
A cycle of life to another,
In the universe of ageless wonders.

THE ARTISTICALLY KNOWN

I felt pity
For those words
Not grown
In beautiful inks
Wasted by its own
To be seen by many
And by the world
Unknown.

Did I forget
How old I am
To be sown?

I crave for more

Unquenchable thirst
The longing for sunrise
In moments before dawn.

Pity

Did I really understand?
The profound meaning of passion.

Love
Hatred
Life

Death
And the
Unknown

It's a beautiful glance
The perfect art of words
Poetry is known.

THE ART OF CREATION

We are small creatures in a wide world
So little to occupy a crowded earth
What is our worth, what can we contribute
When our presence is not valued…

Have we asked ourselves?
The purpose of our conception
A tiny insect may have a reason
To fulfill God's given life-cycle….

The mathematics of life is parallel
For everything have its reasons
A love and hate that collides
Turns out to have a happy ending

An ugly pupa into a beautiful butterfly
A tiny bud that blossoms into a flower
Grasses that make the surroundings green
Trees that calm the storm from raging…

So many things we see or not seen
Designed that no scholar can identify
Not even a poet can recite in a poem
Nor a mathematician can calculate its forms…

Tiny and huge we are shaped
Ugly and beautiful we are made
Each of us has something to contribute
In God's amazing masterpiece
The art of creation!

ONE DAY

Each and every day
From beautiful dawn to dimming gray
No matter how difficult it maybe
I will always find a way to say.

I think of you more each day
The way you speak gently in me
Your smile that brightens my way
Even though I am far away.

The pictures I treasured and kept
Every single memory that I lived
Inspiring me, the strength it gives
Makes this life beautiful to live.

One day, I'll be with you to give
My heart, my soul and my love to share
It's not much but I assure you
Everything in it is enough to keep.

DEEP FRY CHICKEN

I don't need you to like me
Duh, like we're talking either!
We don't have to pretend we're friends
Be kind, if you knew what that means.

Truly, you're so annoying!
With your prolonged sound
Waking me up early in the morning
I don't know why you have to do that thing.

All-day it's exhausting!
You don't come near, just kept running
After I feed you, you just go laying
I know it's cruel but it's our tradition.
.

I really do appreciate your existence
But the painful truth must be unleashed
My stomach is begging for a dish
Fried chicken it is and nothing else.

CHEAP AND FAKE ALIKE

I wonder where they went
After I gave my all and spent
I was broke, alone, and in pain
Everyone is now out of reach
Too busy to help a drowning friend.

I wonder why? Poverty has no friends
Even relatives avoided you in the end
When they knew you had nothing
They seem to forget your real name
Perhaps money is more than fame.

So sad to see people pretend
I'm not asking much if they've none
Being there through thick and thin
Is more than enough to be a friend
To listen, care, comfort, and defend.

Guess now I can tell who really is true
Maybe those people opposite of you
Someone who values real gems in me
Genuine in love, you hear them say "I care."
They do understand while no one else can.

EXACTLY THE SAME

what drives me away
from your begging presence
commonly, without a cent
fowl scent or nonsense.

if you ask why
I will tell you the truth
often told it's no problem
you got very old.

as I told everyone
my responsibility is not
with anyone but my own
cruelly you will agree too.

of course, you do...

I pitied true, poorly you
I share stories sadly, so
here's a food pack chew
for I need to pray for you.

the next day
years did fall
I couldn't walk
so, I crawl.

I don't see you anymore
but everyone does
toss a coin for more.
food pack again I recall.

then I remember what
I did before you died and fall
exactly the same arrogance
people pass by and call!

I AM THE GHOST

I am the ghost that walks upon your lonely dreams.
In each corner and beside your bed is where I
stand.

There's no forgiveness to everything you've done,
for I'm not in God's perfect hand. I am always
there, a feeling that you couldn't possibly
understand.

No need for you to hide or run. I am inside your
thoughts, waiting for you to pull the gun.

Every night I'll wake you like none ever done. Until
justice is mine, you'll suffer like everyone.

WHY?

Often it ends up with why
The feeling stirs cold and fly
Yet sometimes, a moment
Silenced and suddenly cry

Wondering
In countless ways.

Yes, It's the same what if's
And endless thoughts of why's
Is it difficult to ask or to tell
Than to keep it, in labyrinth hell

Why?

Does it satisfiy the truth or
Merely a piece of a word that holds
For someone that still believes
In second chance and hopes

Why? or why not?

SUPPOSEDLY I

Did I need to know
What must be done and
Supposed to be with who?
Maybe I would like a little too.

To be accepted as
Just like everyone
Getting what I need
As few as this one.

We are? is a lie
As good as only I.

Even if I did argue
With the truth and who
Asking questions
Deep inside I already knew.

Then there's YOU
wondering why?

If all ends well
And someone is true.

STRINGLESS

As I walked down the muddy road
Stones sharp and raining in cold
Dirt blots my skin like acid scolds
Asked me why the same color holds.

So, I took shade in your proud lords
They noticed me shivering and bold
Shown me blanket made of shining gold
I became the master's ignorantly fooled.

Nevermind the pages, my past history told
The colors black and white is already old
All fought to be free like those that lost
Slavery now evolves in capturing thoughts.

A less brutal look but more painful chores
None in need of colorful guards to uphold
Willingly they will obey and run as should
Stringless master puppeteers of the world.

THE GRIM AND THE NIGHTINGALE

I played the dirge without any of the light
Strumming guitars, dancing in the night
For one single moment, I never understood
A certain memory could capture my heart cold.

I never speak my love in such melodic chords
If thoughts sound louder than your heart holds
My beauty belongs to the night, where I'm bold
Without freedom nor wings, this cage is off old

For I heard your soul begging just to be reaped
The distance is far and yet too close I kept
My silence will always remain a noble mystery
Until you came and made this heart again beat.

If you're the music that death dare to speak
Let me be the lyric that sings your heartaches
For we're both destined in this night we break
A harmony of souls, not creatures that seek.

FADING COLORS

Where did the colors go?
All that is left, I struggled so
I miss the way they were
Those days you just stood there.

The sunny bluish heavenly sky
Where birds used to fly by
That joyful sound of your voice
Even sometimes annoys me so.

The deep red, painted in my heart
Where every beat longs to survive
That almost every day I did strive
Just to see you in these arms alive.

And the color gray of the moonlight
Where I hide my pain and tearful eye
For every color brings meaning to my life
You became my light that shines.

BEING WITH YOU

Being with you I grow weak
At the same time easy to speak
You understand my troubles
And made me smile, if able.

We are friends, one of a kind
Maybe not the best of it
And quite uniquely different
Still, we talked like soulmates.

Miles apart, one click is a start
From messenger to post we share
It has been a while, I guess but
You choose to stay and be here.

We had countless happy days
And also moments with sad tears
Our friendship comes deep and deeper
From dusk till dawn, our bond appears.

One day I know you'll be blessed
For the kindness, you did for me
I may or may not be with you someday
But I'll always be here when you need me.

For a friend true and one of a kind
Being with you is the best in my life.

STREET DOGS NOT MEN

We compete for a single price
Racing like street dogs we fight
A certain feeling that collides
Seeking gratitude and affirmation
From someone's dream, we derived.

Again and again, still the same idea
The hole and looping system to find
A soulmate that fits like a slave in mind
Expectations we seek, to be deprived
Instantly we move on, like a fast drive.

So, thoughts fly?
There must be
Much better
Than this
Stinky thinking night.

Forty years and bar happy now gone dry
None can be found in everyone's eye
Nevertheless, that regrets sinks in
The mirror doesn't lie with sagging skin
The street dog will now die alone in vain.

MOON RIVER

In mountains underneath the moon
Comes a birthstone that springs at home
Like a river flows in crooked path
Miles away and finally rest into the sea
Bear witness by the moon and the stars.

From each beginning, a glimpse of light
A single journey and encounters of life
No matter how rough the water and tides
Every distinct experience taught us to fight
In a pathway, we derived our strength to survive.

Our quest in the river wild goes beyond
As we tasted every curve, falls, and rides
Touching the stones and earth as we go
A new experience in every travel we knew
Some might hurt us, heal, and leaned as we do.

As time fades and go, we became wiser too
In every drop of morning dew as we knew
That the storm has passed and the rainbow show
Like darkness will soon perish in a new sunrise
As we understand the purpose of our own lives.

The fountain and the source of divine life
The cycle of planets, the mystery of far beyond
Living creatures, crawling and flying up above
The air we breathe and the love we share
All these things can be found in the timeline of life.

IF ONLY, I WONDER WHY?

If only
There's a way
To undo things
I did it already.

If only
I realized things
Before I acted wrongfully
Surely, I will never ever
Let you go and cry.

If only
I could give you
Everything
Those things you
Often dreamed of
My prayers and hope
Are no longer needed.

If only
I understand it before
Not After.

These reasons
This alibi
Pride.
Lies
Never-ending
Long talks and
Wonder whys.

Be ended in one
Single whole
Heartedly
Honest line.

"I'm sorry but
I still love you so".

If only
That's enough
To say.

Will you stay
Give it another try
Or rather say
Goodbye?

INNERMOST

Come, feel the innermost
A token of love without any cost
Be gentle, kind, and be at peace
Smile and give all your best.

Beauties we must learn to enjoy
Feel the breeze that brings joy
The sun will rise after this night
Those you fought will hold on tight.

A light shall shine after this fight
Deep inside you know this is right
The beauties and the charming lads
Friends, relatives, and families are glad.

Don't isolate yourself, go and depart
The innermost lives deep in your heart
Don't waste your time holding your grudge
Let go of your worries, just enjoy the fudge!

VENGEANCE SHALL REAP

Climb and sway above the earth
Hang your head upon ropes of death
Push your heart over the edge
Scream like your losing your grip
The fallen shall rise from the abyss.

All souls shall beg and be reaped
Like prey, run and hide like sheep
Watch as I'll take your last breath
Purge this night, angels of death
The forgotten shall rise from sleep.

I will deliver every book and prophecies
None will escape my grudge and lifetime hate
Vengeance shall play upon your begging creep
The gods will not be there to save your place
I will burn them all even your precious pet.

I will not show mercy, the serpent is unleashed
My venom is deadlier than a thousand blades
Scalp every inch of your skin and baked
You'll walk the earth on bloody feet
As you slowly die, I will laugh and be great.

I AM SORRY, IF I'VE SAID GOODBYE

Maybe it would best for both of us
It's no longer healthy and love don't last
We exhausted ourselves so much
Curse, profanities, and outcast
For that, it hurts a lot.

Is it an illusion or merely a game
A tricky feeling of having someone
To fill our emptiness and loneliness
Whatever it is none to gain but this
Or perhaps I just give too less.

Am I blind knowing you're not mine
A forbidden love that becomes a circus
Funny it's supposed to be, a private affair
I don't know how to make it sound fair
Better or bitter we must end.

I am sorry if I must say goodbye
Hoping we found each other peace
My heart just know it would be best
Seeking someone that truly cares
For our love seems no longer exist.

ARISE

Scents hidden
Thoughts of the other side
Beyond those clouds
I am waiting for a ride.

Enter the realms
Gamers, sinners, and saints
Travelers of the wild
Let's put this agony to end.

Remember this domain
Passers lost their names
Forgotten and unforgiven
All of you at least the same.

Slithers of twilight
Hearts of fallen cried
Fiery rage and pride died
Darkness will now decide.

Yet, it's too late for me
No horns on this head
Know who am I, will be
Thrones will arise.

I JUST HATE THIS FEELING

I just hate this feeling
It has a way of deceiving
Intimately sweet cravings
Crept and stripped my being.

It dwells deep into my thoughts
It makes me imagine things
Made every promise broken
And yet, It still does allure me!

Oh, why?
You're such a super player
I wish I couldn't see you again
Evaporate! Go melt! I don't care.

But you don't give up that easy
I don't want you here anymore
Please stop tempting me
I'll never be your favorite slave!

PIECE BY PIECE

Shattered pieces
Each holds deep
Begging soul
Losing breathe.

Asking why?
Over and over, it hurts.

Instances
Past hunts, creeps
Broken and unheard
Lay, hushed on the bed!

Wounds are so deep.
Unseen, unsealed.

Silence then came
Smiles no longer the same
Changed. Hanging
Heart fragmented, broken.

What a peaceful dark fading sky!
I felt it all, falling one by one.

MISERY

Gestures, long lost friend
Unexpectedly came.
Farewell, torments, and the same
The night is in debt, paradox
Mazes of what has been.

Forbid! Let me crawl, it's late
Mourn, is no more.
Farewell perhaps leave
But surely you'll see me
Beheaded.

Redeem'd.
Grim be silent, reap!
None were fed
Neither be freed
Or longer needed.

Live like the dead.
Like you believe.
Lies you hide.
Love deprived.

BREATHING IN A FOG

I breathe fire
Without flame
Inhaling in hate.

Fractured.

Heart heavy
Mourning late
Silently standing.

No tears.

Presumption
Phenomenon
Cold storm.

Death.

Fears
Bleed, then
Solemn stillness.

I escaped.

Resistance is fragile
Like fractured bone, itches
So, I breathe in the fog.

And did fade.

A PIECE OF BREAD

Never had you heard
A child begs for bread
Almost malnourished
Knocking on a window shield.

Sunken sulking silent eyes
Smelly rotten almost cried
Sack on the side, palms open wide
Drenched in sweat, foul breath.

Running naked always afraid
Abused at night, no one cares
Empty head, starving heart
Sleeping on the cold street.

They are the true poets
The metaphor of your sheets
Pushing pencil you sketch
For a Nobel prize, you get.

Oh, please educate me.

What does it mean?
To do none the same
If your human enough
And not numb insane!

IN SUCH PRESENCE

I came to rest and made peace
In such a beautiful presence
Where nature is in deep serenity
None the less, wind caressing free
And the breeze heard by waving trees.

Here I stand, alone in the bridge of art
Where the scent of a hazy morning, smiles
Upon the heart-shaped lilies of still water
I cast away my burden, regaining my strength
In a quiet way of saying, "I will never give in!"

The battles being fought behind
Uncertainty of what lies beyond
Choices that will be made in between
By this very moment, beheld by heart
For everything is seen in clarity, I defy.

In such a presence,
I may now rest.

ROSES ARE RED

To speak love by its own language
Upon the colors of those who wait
The kind of courage that dares to speak
Let it be known, be true. If it bleeds.

Paint the petals as deep as maroon red
For those who hold beauty be pierced
By painful thorns, no scars shall be healed
In the heart and soul of true love itself.

To every sense and breath of those lips
Eyes and smiles which inherit beauty
Undefined by wonders of my own universe
I give such pleasure to my losing self.

For I had not known who am I unless
Be drown in the deepest arch of an abyss
In the garden of my innermost affection
Roses are red, for your love as long as I live.

ROAD LESS TRAVELLED

Never had I known
Deny each lesson being sown
Neither travel the world
This late that could not be grown.

By such a foolish idea, I adorned.
I knew it's a way and saw.

Yet I long to be in it, in any way
They often say it's stupidity
From this sagging carcass found
A child filled with craving curiosity.

Does idiocy capture me?
Or aging is quite dull, I say.

For years it was taught
Educated, wise and tough
But what time does bought?
Grumpy old cannot be told!

I wrote books before my legacy
Preparing funeral before my day.

So, this is how the story ends
A road less traveled by men
Did I stay that long?
I felt like becoming the road.

MAN-MADE OF GOLD

Never had I walked with heavy shoulders
From this boulevard of painful regrets
As I look upon the lights, waving in hates
Heavy pockets are full of paper sheets.

The night is deep but home seems don't wait
Walking along in this cold street, I breath
Regrets often found, even if I will lose myself
Destination put me in a place that doesn't exist.

I am old, my children are old, everyone is old
Gold are many as I have told, as they foretold
It is quite bold to tell how much did I really hold
Treasure brings no pleasure when you're old.

Truly, it still does in some ways if you insist
But it can never buy me back my youthful days
Nor companionship of the one who really cares
Money is good, if only it serves the right purpose.

So, here I am walking at night filled with gold
Looking fine outside but never did I ever sold
That one of these days, I'll be buried in this cold
Leaving behind every penny that I love for good.

DAYTIME FIREFLIES

It rains like
Summer snow
Flying on air
In early June
Dusty white glow.

Dancing
In the wind blows
Invading the earth
We don't know
If only you saw
How amazing
They flew!

I am slowly
Beginning to learn
How wonderful it is
From each smallest
Things are seen
Blossoms love
In the wind.

Let it fly high
Up above the sky
And befall
Everywhere
Anywhere
Like showering
Seeds of hope
For all who cope.

So, let it be sown
Be grown
Be beautiful
For all mankind.

MAID OF HONOR

If only I could, I probably would
Make ways to know you better
From those days you just stood by
And as I pass down the aisle.

I couldn't barely speak of you than
For words found no strength within
Maybe priorities have a way of denying
What I had for you is truly pure loving.

For years, I kept this incarcerated
Beyond those things I had shown
A secret that I feared to be known
I am nobody and for that I'm unknown.

Perhaps it's quite too late to be spoken
As I stand beside your bride in silence
The maid of honor I am, for loving you so
But who am I to take away those smiles.

Indeed you deserved to be with the best
It doesn't matter anymore if I let it go
For this day, might be too cruel for me
But how can I deny the happiness in you?

FINALLY FOUND ME

Where did
I use to lay?
in the nest,
the pastures?
or of grey?

As words were spoken:
I found freedom,
To play
From each tales
And footprints

When once upon a time
The morning
That was fine as today
When sorrow finds
No reason to stay

Then it spoke
In the gentle breeze and said
Life finally found me,
When I'm gone astray
In a picture

Perfectly made
Out of clay

THE FALLEN

Upon the arrows that pierce
Backstabbing foes, words and blades
I kneel down begging on your knees
For strength drained, tired and in pain
I am a knight, dying in the battlefield

As I lay down on this ground
I grieve, looking up to heaven
Without a single murmuring sound
Then I asked, where's heaven?
When darkness is found all around

And I tried my best to resist
But I'm all alone, my shield bleeds
Where my heart longs and craves
In a land far away from home, slayed.
This is my curse, a never-ending slave

This is arrogance without honor
A retaliation of long-lost realization.
Unforgivable. A taste of prolonged agony
As I depart on this lonely road of perdition
Let this quill find a peaceful place to rest

DYING ALONE
(Free Verse)

Somehow I am no longer there
But some memories are still here

A dusty place where I slept
In a small space, I could hardly stand
And eyes looking at a small window
Where I am far, far away from sight

True, it's my fault I was there
Lucky for you, you're not here
Sadly they couldn't be anyway
But maybe that's what it has to be

Life is not the same anymore
Everyone has priorities of their own

Perhaps it's meant to be
Or not?

And then, I began to understand
How I wasted life at one glance

But, again
It doesn't matter anymore

If I had changed and I'm already gone
Nature is cruel and people are too
I guess that's what they do best

Again, it doesn't matter anymore
Sooner or later I'm gonna die here

But if I could...

To make it up
And do things right

Even chances
Are quite small

I do.

BEAUTIFUL DEATH
(Free Verse)

I tremble.
Feeling afraid,
By such judgment
I bleed.

By such thinking
I died.
The strong allure of
The unknown

My silence
Speaks courage

My soul
My life
Remains

A mystery.

A beautiful
Death before
Sunrise

OUT OF THE BLUE
(Awdi Gywydd - Welsh Quatrain)

Out of the blue, I died true
Colorless rue says I'm done!
Feeling no longer the same
The truth did aim, yet undone

No goodbyes, nor tears in eyes
Silently I. Clueless, why?
I shut the door and did hide
Look like Mr.Hyde, feeling shy

After I heard words that pierce
Lingers in ears, what else there?
All are same not even close
So, let it loose! none is here

Dusk is closing to dark scales
Gossip and tales, for the girls
Believe me nothing worth to kill
All of them, ill and just twirl

I think I deserved better
Not a bitter, sadistic affair
For out of the blue I think
Before I sink, this is fair!

TRICKY STRONG
(Blitz)

Lovestruck
Love is tricky
Tricky is difficult
Tricky heart
Heart to own
Heart that mourns
Mourn for love
Mourn alone
Alone in the dark
Alone in the moon
Moon and stars
Moon that cries
Cries for hate
Cries for betrayed
Betrayed by words
Betrayed by men
Men crash
Men for cash
Cash to hold
Cash that burns
Burns your home
Burns your future
Future in time
Future against the world
World of deceits
World falls down
Down with you
Down and crippled
Crippled and learned
Crippled and yet stand
Stand to fight

Stand for the right
Right to live
Right to laugh
Laugh the past
Laugh that last
Last a lifetime
Last one to have
Have and not had
Have and be glad
Glad to be loved
Glad to love
Love your worst
Love your past
Past is past
Past makes you strong
Strong not to let go
Strong to think
think…
go…

THEY CAME, THEY TOOK
(Free Verse)

Like hungry wolves in winter
They invade our homes and land
Eat among our children with guns
Reapers of trees, oceans, and man

They came, they saw
They knew what they had done
They are the gods, our death dealers
And yet they, you did none

What makes you think you're human?
While you enjoyed watching your fellow
Slaughtered by the wolves of man
You pitied and still sat there,
And again you did none

Our children beg
Our women mourned and raped
Our men became slaves
Nevertheless hopeless dead

And yet again, you did none?

One day
Maybe not today
The wolves will come again
It doesn't matter when
Or what season ends

They will reap you off

As what they did to our homes
Perhaps...
They will come for you too

And yet again,
You will ask the same
Why everyone did none?

THE WORTH OF PROMISES
(Free Verse)

I never lose sight of hope
Each day I did my best to cope
Even though keeping you is difficult
I guess it's no longer my fault

I'm trying to understand why
Why promises are often broken
Perhaps for some, it's not important
The value of honor and words

Love is made of promises
Something we hold on to each other
For those who truly trust you
It's the only thing they hope for

Keeping them bring loyalty and more
The stronger your bond will become
Much the worth of who you are
And the person who awaits at hand

Breaking it constantly
Is a plain and simple rotten lies
Tell me if words are not kept
What makes a man?

I guess, none

AND THEN

I've been to the highest
Mountain peak and swim down
The deepest ocean floor
Still, I don't know what
I am truly looking for

Paddle in the wildest, river wild
Maneuvering each difficult drive
To the point where I barely survived
For I've noticed it all is just a ride
And found no one who shares at my side

And then...

You came into my unsteady troubled life
Makes my mountain peak easy to climb
And walk down the shore wearing a smile
You made the river wild fun to endure
Truly you're my angel worth loving more

FOR ALL I AM, IS YOURS

For those wacky times
That you took me out of the blue
As you kiss my cheeks

For that precious moment
Which makes this life complete
As you kiss my lips

For those tears, I shed
That you spend time to listen
Let me say thank you

For all the sacrifices made
That we strived hard to beat
Let me offer you my heart

For making me worth having
That special feeling I never did had
Let me stay by your side

For your gentle hands that care
That kept me warmth at lonely nights
Let me share my soul with you

And for all the things being done
That I never knew you did for me
Let me offer you a lifetime of love

BLUE STREAKS

as I lay down,
awake at dawn

.

all I hear
is nothing
but my own
whispering
in cold air
and mourn
a symphony
meant
for my dying
moon

.

knowing
the sun
will rise up
soon

I think
it's just
fascinating
to swear
where
the outcome
is already known
the scenery
are getting more
predictable

.

the message
is clear,
I own my own
but I still cling on
someone's
unknown

.

rhythm is like
a beat
while my heart
burns
at last streaks
shown
I am, wishfully
Will not soon
Be alone

.

TORMENTED

I felt the burning heat of my soul
The agony that screams deep within
With every flesh and skin that wears out
I think of vengeance from now and then

Did I suffer more than enough to mourn
When does it weigh much than your own
Heaven stood there laughing at my bones
Am I the sinner you wish never been born

I will never understand your righteous tone
Perhaps we both had a path dark and doomed
You see now, you end up with light and gloom
While I'm whipped hard and left damn alone

Never I pitied myself by these arrogant morons
Death will come sooner than my miserable moon
For grief and mourn will at least let me be home
And then all shall be gathered in my coldest tomb

BLACK CHRISTMAS

Glittering white fairy dust,
Black heaven for the outcast.
As I look up above,
I saw it torn apart.
Lonely heart beating so fast,
Tears fell out and pain that last.

Caroling sounds in a distant land,
No angels came down like blondes.
Idiots said, "it's Christmas eve
my greedy lads, why look so sad?"
Perhaps, people often get mad.

A blossoming house like cotton buds,
As the trees bear fruits through the glass.
See these walls painted in bloody arts,
As the melody played in mourning dusk.
It's black Christmas at long last.

Ring the church bell three times,
A quiet dinner with candlelit and wine.
Wear tux as dark as the night,
For tomorrow we will all die like rats.

SOMETIMES

Sometimes we need
to stay away from people,
for them to able to grow
and be a better person.

Sometimes we need,
to hurt them to be awakened.
To make them understand,
the difference between reality
and foolish dreams.

Sometimes we need,
To understand
even others don't.
Sometimes we need,
To let go and move on
even it hurts us most.

Sometimes.

A LOVE TO LAST

From giggling smiles comes,
A beautiful morning.
Contentment of having her comes,
A lifetime of joy.

Even years may pass,
Or how boring her day was.
Kiss her, make her feel loved,
After all, that's all she asked.

Find time to remember,
That promises are meant to last.
Argument, jealousy, and childish acts,
Are spices to consider not reasons
To break her fragile heart.

For you once asked for her love,
It's only right not to break it apart.
Nevermind your ridiculous wants,
For love has always been
A selfless act!

CHASE HER

Chase the sun,
that brightens your day.

make her laugh,
make her stay,
make her beautiful,
each and in every way.

Chase the moon,
that precious moment
when you're both alone.

kiss her forehead,
for the wonderful thoughts
she gave.
kiss her eyes,
for the path and the road
she showed.
kiss her ears,
for the time
she spent listening.
kiss her lips,
for the love
you both shared.

Chase her,
even she's near.
Chase her,
even she's yours.
Chase her,

make her fall in love
every single day.

UNTITLED

Have I not done good enough?
To be left wounded this way,
For I give it all, and yet betrayed still.

When will I see my heart rejoice again?
Dancing in heaven without pain,
I am lost in the pouring of rain.

Will love be sweeter,
This time around?
Does the bond enslave me?
Fate is faith,
But will you be here
This late.

Too many questions.
And so many answers,
I refused to know.

My vow often hurts me so.

Am I selfish?
Am I not beautiful?
Then why,
Why you cheated.

Now,

I am nameless.
I am what they say I am.
I am untitled to be entitled.

Am I?

LABYRINTH SMILE

The bones were shaped for me
As I stand before the heavens today
Rough stones piercing deep within
Waiting for the rain to touch my skin
What lovely eyes staring
Suffering without pain.

The tides came as many times
Teasing the sand grains on the shore
Still, here I am still waiting for someone
Truthful enough in their hearts to adore
Bleed for me, I stand forevermore

For what love has offered me
Sorrow often knocked at my door
Dare I should be afraid or fled
At times of spring and autumn falls
When you're already here with me
Waiting to be embraced after all

And then, the sun smiles,
At the labyrinth of our longing souls.

PAPER BOAT

I fold it ten times more,
Seen it sailing on the shore.
A paper written made of thoughts,
It is something I never did buy
Truly, funny and odd!

Even memories have faded,
A melting sheet into the water cold.
As dusk aged a thousand years old,
The world never knew me and
How life was being foretold.

Yet, the journey came near
While the horizons drown in fears.
It shrinks down in tiny beautiful tears
And the thoughts of you were there,
Written in blotted ink that sails.

The destination was lost,
As it sinks deeper in dark abyss.
Paper boat made of thoughts,
Buried underneath the tides
Waiting to be missed.

ONE HEART

Soon the sun
Will rise.
What price shall I pay?
For having a dawn
Made of you and me,
Truly I am blessed.

Uncertain of what
This day,
Or whatsoever
Life may bring?

I give it all
Just for a moment,
For you to stay
Beneath my wings.

A different time.
In a beautiful winter cold
Having what I could really hold,
A love that heals my soul.

Kiss me, my love,
Be the flame that warms
My longing heart
As I quench all my thirst
In your loving lips.

FORSAKEN

Let me mourn to the death of no one
Cry harder for I am no longer that girl
I made it difficult to understand but
Believe me, I give it all at a second chance

Never have I seen beautiful moments
Suddenly perish in such painful deceit
Never have I try just to be judged this way
For tongue never rest in agonizing dismay

Why can't I be happy neither you maybe
Does God forsaken what has left in me
Oh, how cruel your vulgar of power plays
You stab me ten times than yesterday

Tell me does fear stronger than love
If faith is something to set us apart
Then I find destiny only a one big fat lie
For love is not love until you give it away.

LANDAS NG BUHAY

Gaano man kahaba ang paglalakbay
Gaano man kabigat ang inaakay,
Gaano man karami ang hadlang
May Diyos na laging nagbabantay.

Sa maraming taong inaalay --
Sa paghihirap, pag-uusig at mga ligalig
Sa pagmamahal sa kapwang kumakalinga,
Namamalagi ang gabay sa ating puso.

Laging isipin ang iginawad na pagpapatawad
Sapagkat ang ating Ama'y mapaglingap.
Bukod tanging dahilan kaya tayo'y kaanib pa
Sa loob ng kawan, may pag-iingat Niya.

Sa landas nitong buhay tayo'y iniligtas Niya,
Ang katotohanang hindi kailanman maiwagsi.
Salubungin ang bawat sandali ng may galak
Dahil sa kanyang pagpapala, may pagmamahal.

THE DEMON I FOUND

I found a penny made of fancy gold
In the street where everybody is fooled
The sun is dimming there in bloody cold
As I catch my breath ten times fold
No wonder no one seems to get old.

In the mountain tops, I strolled
The wolves are howling for food
The old man said the city is not good
Evil exists in this part of the world
So, I step down trying to unfold.

As I looked up high in the clouds
I try to make it better with the crowd
In the weakest sound, I did shout out
Not even the earthworms applaud
Out of dismay, I gave it all away.

Sunday came all singing the same
The preacher said the demons are to blame
So, I looked for one out of this lonely game
Never I understand how deceitful I've gone
And the mirror replied you're that man.

COLORLESS

I stumble upon a beauty
Far beyond these walls
As it lay down and crawl
You'll see it stunningly tall.

Did I say not even proud at all
You can distinguish the smiles
Fearless and yet so adorable
By any means do tell the bull.

But men judged it by color
Sad to say a weakness they call
In silence couldn't argue more
So let it be and let them rule.

If tribes are made of gold
Why silver all men have forged
If a beautiful rose is painted in red
Then green men must be told.

THE MAN AND THE SHADOW

The light glimpse out of nowhere
And the door was dared to open
Here you see a man being silenced
By the shadow, he holds in years.

Sadness was worn
And tries to bury it deep under
Never been shown by any
That heart seems lost and wander.

Then grief came along with tears
Look at the mirror no man came near
Yet, it did calmly whispered in the ear
"Did the shadow followed you here?"

I think there's a slight mistake
The man now dares to stand and speak
Changes were made here out of the lake
And the shadow replied, "what did I take?"

DANCING IN THE WIND

From the moment I did fall
I was dancing without a floor
In every tune of music I sway along
And did prolong that lonely song.

For years I've been part of they
Happily watching below with glee
Never thought this day would come
That I fell down in lifeless play.

The heat seems to dry my skin brown
As I lay sad on this hallowed ground
Waiting for heaven to lift me up
Yet, the dirt holds my body tight around.

So I stay still and the same as everyone
No tears may roll for my heart is no more
If you asked me how did my life play for all
My answer is dancing in the wind and fall.

UNDERNEATH THE RAIN

Out of sight, it stands here with who
In dripping dew of darkness and blue
Barely knew and nowhere else to go
The fallen has no heavenly true.

Seems they forgot where I am too
Underneath the rain that crippled me so
For I could no longer feel my heart sing
That thing I used to do, fade with you.

What is worth when birds no longer flew
No whispering cold breeze on summer day
I could no longer see the river that flows
Even the flowers dried and died with you.

A broken spirit hides away in the sunshine glow
The day may enlighten those who never knew
Ask the dusk and unmask what is true
Even if the rain at night stops I still do.

THE SILENT CREEK

As I sat down along the dock
In a place made of harden rocks
I heard no one but the ticking of a clock
And the emptiness that haunts back.

Near the creek made of stagnant water
I had felt the deep abyss down under
Weary eyes look upon the empty boat
Saying no paddle in a sad written quote.

To whom do I say my last farewell words
I spend it waiting in the shade of winter cold
Avoiding the sun that burns my sagging skin
While the moon mocks my longing dreams.

Still, I refused to fade in the dying horizons
My heart is tired but my soul hopes for one
A single beautiful moment of being truly loved
Before the last breath be taken from above.

A SPECIAL PLACE

There's a certain part of me
Deep inside you will always be
It's not made of lies or fantasy
Something pure, not ecstasy.

I do not know how to explain it
Truly it blossoms so beautifully
Like a seed that grows slowly within
That meant for my soul to mend.

Perhaps it's magical or maybe not
But I love the way it does make me feel
The wonders of what's true and for real
A kind of, that I honestly care.

Surely for some, it's meaningless
Another poetic metaphor if they insist Infatuation,
love, what if's or what else
The truth is you made that special place.

BLEED

I never thought that it would bleed
But it did that day you decided to leave
Dripping without a wound inside my head
The questions why is it so cruel instead.

Have I not done enough to be worthy, for I
Sold my soul for you each and every day
I pour it all like nothing else could fall
Even my heart will only beat by your call.

Your absence and my act of despair
Reflects in a thousand poetic words
As I mourn in great longingness here
Silence is filled with anguish and tears.

As the streaks of dawn share my doom
I began to understand the sun is born
For my farewell will always to the moon
Love will survive and soon be grown.

THE CRYINGH MOON

Once I sang a song
Out of the blue
As I sat alone
In the wilderness of you
Broke my soul and
Brittle heart in two
You said one day
It will heal and just go
Sad to know but somehow
It's not true.

As I wander around and
Beyond the crowds
Beautiful flowers blossoms
Out of the dew
I told them stories of how sad
It did finally flew
Amazingly they pity
My broken wings too
I tried to let it go but instead
I hurt them so.

Never knew why
I am so cruel though
Lost in so many faces
I found in you
Do dreams of love curse me

When it's turning blue
Every night I looked up
In the stars of who
Only to find out
The moon was crying too.

WRITER'S BLOCK

I don't know
What"s wrong
All I ever wanted
Is to write
A few dreams
And your song.

But nothing
Came out
No words or thoughts
To dwell nor to tell
Dreams are sealed
I knock my head
No inks did bleed.

So, I just
Rest and lay down
Next to you
Without a word.

Silently
I gazed into your eyes
Gently kissed
And hugged you
Tight.

And said
Darling, you're
My sweetest
Writer's block.

FOR ALL I HAVE IS YOU

Each day I wake up
Then what do I see?
It's the same morning
As I woke up yesterday.

All the routines and worries
Cloudy crowds or sunny play
Somehow, powerless to change
I can still make it a happy day.

All I got, everything I had
Whatsoever is here, is what I have
Everything is real right now to me
Will eventually pass my way.

I don't mind much of what
I've been through and used to do
Knowing what's important and true
And for that, I'll spend my time with you.

Indeed, I can't predict what's ahead
I know someone is guiding my head
Knowing there it is, I found my peace
And the sole contentment in loving you.

MOM'S LAST WORDS

My dear daughter
I am quite old
Before I perish
Cherish what I've told.

All the lessons
I've learned
Will not be exactly
Like your own
Our path maybe
Different but
There are some
Needing to be known.

Always remember
My words with you.

Love your family and
Be loyal to your home
Trust the people
Who trusted you
Don't cheat or lie
Just be true
Surely, they will
Respect you.

The world isn't always
Nice and wonderful
Some people got hurt too
They may be deceitful
And very rude sometimes

Afraid of what you might do
But it doesn't mean
There's no goodness
Inside their hearts
Even so.

Always try to be humble
Forgive them if you must
Pray to God even if others don't
Never give up your faith
For you'll never be lost
And ever be alone.

UNDER THE TREE

I think of things you used to say
That I was not being born yesterday
And all that you could only do for me
Will be wrapped under the tree.

It's been a wild chase to see
At some point every single day
No cage but feels like I'm not free
And my thoughts often turn to you.

I did cry until it runs out
Wandered alone down many paths
And shiver at night in the corridors
While asking the moon where's the door.

I know this is not your wish for me
You only wanted it to end peacefully
Perhaps it's time to mend and say
Better wrap you up too under the tree.

TEARS GONE DRY

I am drowning feeling insane
Nowhere else to go but down below
Tears went dry and I could no longer cry
Hoping you never did say goodbye.

I know you can't be with me now
Somehow I wish you never did go
That kind of hope broke me so
For I still wish you were still mine too.

All my life once I live it for only you
Everything I did I entrusted to you
My thoughts, my heart, and soul is you
Even that I guess is not enough for you.

Time doesn't totally heal me
Sometimes I scream without a sound
For with you, there's nothing I found
While my love longs and still around.

BEAUTIFUL IN MY EYES

You're the beauty among the stars
The light that guides my journey
Who speaks in my heart like honey
And sting me like a crazy bee.

Like a sweet rose with red petals
That allure my sight in the wild
Or a ghost at night and hunts
My heart in mysterious heights.

I could reach the highest sky
And swim the deepest ocean
No matter how rough and tough
The road may be, gladly I will be.

I wish I could tell you all of these
Without shaking my knees
Truly wishing for your grace
For my life is meant for this.

Bless me with your affectionate love
For I need nothing more than a kiss
Hold me like no one ever did before
For you're my heaven I'm craving to taste.

NUMB

Am I really a fool
Believing that one day
My love for you
Bounces back like a ball.

Mystery if they call
I've tried to buy it all
Chocolates, flowers and
Against heaven may fall.

I wish you noticed
See me through the years
Much more than a friend
I did love you till it ends.

You made me realized
How numb you are my friend
Not deserving to be loved
For your heart is not mend.

So I said, goodbye to you
But the feeling didn't just go
Better stay I guess
And then love you more
Much more than a friend.

THE CLOWN

You'll never see my tears
Neither looks of shivering fears
I am the clown of a happy face
Your confession of the problem phase.

I will show no weakness but grace
Everything has a solution, I wish
My words speak like "I know this",
Then just smiles when it's a mess.

I pretend to be strong when I'm weak
Laugh at danger while it almost breaks
You'll never see me beg nor be afraid
My wounds are deep, yet I don't bleed.

I had to be, I have to be brave
Everyone depends and count on me
No matter how cruel this world can be
I'll always be the clown for my family.

PASSENGERS

Years may pass
But I still remember you
That day you and I met
How we talked in that seat.

As we traveled along our way
To a place meant to set us free
We smiled, laughed and then I said
The trip doesn't make me sad today.

You're witty, smart and quite friendly
Maybe the connection was weird
So awkward but I like it too instantly
And found comfort in stories of yesterday.

Somehow the hours seem too short
I really don't want that moment to end
But the destination is reached, my friend
So we have to say our sad goodbyes once again.

Too late to cry and to remember
Perhaps we're not meant to be together
For that was the last time I found him
And the seat remains empty forever.

ROCK, PAPER OR SCISSORS

I know this will be hard
But my friend, please do try
Though others don't see as you do
Act as if, you understand them too.

Just because they hated you
Being judged by people you knew
Deep inside, truth shines through
And for that, they envy you so.

In times of strangers, be cautious
In times of friendship, be picky
In times of relationship, be wise
In times of restless foes, be steady.

Talk nice when you're challenged
Cooldown and know your timing
Strike when you're tired of running
Vengeance served best when it's cold.

But if peace you seek
Find a home inside your heart
But if rock sinks, paper floats
No need for a scissor to cut them both.

INSANITY

It speaks like the tongue of the wicked
See it fly beyond what you expected
Play the words, sway, turn, and twisted
In every corner of your head, it existed.

Fireflies, lies, ties that blinded
Sweet tears, ears, hears that shaded
There you find the same quotes blended
Then, tell yourself its reality has ended.

Tango with your ego that hasn't landed
Fight when you knew it's not needed
Beg, hug, bang where you beheaded
And finally, start talking in your head.

Think...

What's being normal anyway?
Whatever defines your philosophies.
Call it linguistically crazy, but
It's just temporary insanity.

BEING A MAN

If being a man requires
Hitting and cheating a woman
I choose to be
A woman.

If being a man requires
Not to do household chores
I choose to be
A woman.

If being a man requires
Not protecting family
I choose to be
A woman.

If being a woman requires
Loving a man
Then I choose to learn to be
A man rather than
A woman.

ANG HULING TAG-ARAW

Parang kailan lang
Pinagmamasdan kitang natutulog
Himbing na tila'y pagod na pagod at
Umaasa sa muli mong paggising.

Sa mga alaalang napakasaya
Biglang gumuho sa aking mga mata
Hiling ko'y dingin man lang sana
Bago bumigay ang iyong hininga.

Sa bawat patak ng aking luha
Pangalan mo ang siyang sinasambit
Sa mga gabing may lungkot at pait
Diyos lang ang tanging nakakarinig.

Parang huling takip silim
Unti unting ika'y nagpapaalam
Sa iyong ngiting bakas ang sakit
Sana'y ako nalang ang pumipikit.

Hanggang bumigay ang langit
Tila isang masamang bangungot
Pumanaw kang puno ng lungkot
At dumilim habang ako'y pumalaot.

Tadhana nga ba ang maiwan?
Ganun pa man tinuruan ng tama
Ang isang napakagandang biyaya
Ang pagmamahal na nagpapalaya.

UNDERNEATH THAT TREE

Beneath that green tree
Lies heaven with the color gray
Weeping silence goes astray
For things you once portrayed.
Speechless and yet gripping down
As you look up and none is around
Tears falling slowly without a sound
Losing faith is like a hallowed ground.
Love is lonely often said by many
Poem blossoms even poets disagree
Words are spoken, not in reality
Vivid memories will hunt you one day.
Years may pass, even today
To heal wounds is not that easy
As it comes across and sways
Remember you once cried and died
Underneath that old lonely tree.

SHED, I

Speak, the tongue did I?
The dark bleed so, the sky.
Embrace the emptiness,
I long to touch your eyes.
Where's the light? As I,
Believe in your lies.
Struggle, the thoughts of I?
Everything seems fine,
As angels look like butterflies.
Denials. Lies. Lies. Lies.
Yet, I'm still surprised.
Shed, the shade replies.
Tears, blossoms, and fly.
Kiss, the hug had died.
Why, why and why?
Did I care? More than I?

MOONDANCE

I love the marveling of its light,
The soothing sound that I fight.
Yet, I beg to be with you,
In the glimpse of your eyes.
A captivating scene of
a beautiful soul.
What defines a moonlight?
In the loneliness of life.
The usual voices of lies and smiles.
Our goals, socialize and prize.
Or the rotten truth that sooner we die?
At least,
Let me dance and sway,
For just one last cry.
Perhaps forget who I was,
In the passages of perdition.
A longing for a chance.
To love and be loved.
To kiss and be kissed.
To know my worth.
And simply be happy.

MAYBE I AM

I wish there's more at sea,
As the day passes by and
The sunrise frowns at me.
Yet, here I am.
Breathing and waiting,
If I'm needed to be free.
What awaits this day?
If there's no one left to see,
No music to dance and sway.
Even the birds no longer
Sings our melodies.
Still, I live.
I fight, I fought, I thought
I smiled, I lied and I cried.
The door is open,
There's no chain,
I am free but
Still, I'm too scared to go.

BARELY BREATHING

I am the queen of the dark kingdom,
No people nor a queen to defend.
All I feel is agony and remorseful pain,
My throne is made of sand grains.
I live in the center of wilderness,
Among the cruel and the heartless beast.
No sharp-bladed sword but words,
And my only allies are beyond these walls.
I am destined for damnation,
No token of gratitude or salutations
With limited visual and body motions.
In a soundless dusty box, I remain.
Hear my agonizing voice today.
For someone long forgotten.
Seeking justice, not vengeance.
All I ever needed is to be treated,
As a human being again.

BEAUTIFUL IN BLACK

What draws me close to the fire?
That kind of feeling, I desire.
My gracious, and mysterious
Way of being a woman.
Upon your eyes,
The heat and the cold collide.
Like being in Neverland
Full of magical and wild.
Faceless, I hear only your voice.
All I see in your eyes is your soul,
A tempting way to be drowned, be lost
In the paradise of your lifetime mystery.
I wish I could touch you,
I wish I could kiss you.
I wish you're mine.
I wish we have this moment.
I wish I could redefine
The laws of ancient times.
For us to live freely, without colours
Without tribes and without dimes.

THIRST

There are things better left unsaid,
The kind that sinks deeper in my head.
I don't know if it's right or wrong to crave
As thoughts of you become so weird.
Still, I am denying the truth of what I feed.
Against morality, all odds seem so sweet.
The lonely and the quiet sound of my bed,
Forsaken nights wrecked me in despair.
Humming darkness, as I closed my eyes,
Like a child longing to be cuddled at night.
I grabbed my pillow, wrapped my legs tight
Where's heaven when no angel is at my side?
I've tried to reach you in my dreams,
Not even a tone, silent, without a voice.
Can you hear me? Can you still see me?
I'm all yours, to be touched without noise.

SLAVE

Unhook the chain
From this neck
For the man willing enough
To be your slave
I will give it all
Until I rock and roll
Allowing you to spank
Until my buttons shall fall
Beg for your kiss
Slap me, while I'm trying this
Bend over
Hug you there
Here comes
The missionary wish
Trying my best to please
For the Goddess of beauty
I am the slave of my own
Pleasurable request.

DECEMBER LOVE

Sometimes I saw you
Crying along the way
Weeping in the wounds of June
While begging for May to stay.
July came late and said
Did August made us smile
When September is with you today?
You said, perhaps in October, I will.
Suddenly you remember April
By the shore of reminiscing play
The rivalry of past, present, and yesterday
Blinded you in the days of March.
It's November, hurts you that much
The grieving pain of your loving ghost
When you know December awaits for you
In the longing months of who loves you most.

DEATHLY BRIDE

Perhaps not perfect
The woman inside is weak
All I ever wanted
Maybe the things that are
No longer needed.
I don't seem to understand why
Flowers I brought didn't mean a thing
If you look closer into my eyes
You'll see the fire dying inside
Maybe this love will still survive.
I am deprived of happiness
Betrayed by the only man that
I thought would hold still
What happened to Better or
Mine is only for the worst.
A dose of dripping agony
Like rain on a cold summer day
As the winter froze my way
Into the horizon where
Fading sunset drops away
My hope cries for one more play.

MANNEQUIN

In the street where I used to go,
People talk even if, I do not know.
Between crossroads and alleys too,
A country of strange, strangers grow.
I am the dead, in the romance we do.
Long live the king, the short days blew.
Never seen the sunset did ever glow,
Some nice, naive, and natively lying true.
My dream is high, yet, dragged me to die.
I took this battle in the bed of roses too.
Somehow, I am helplessly feeling so blue.
For you enjoy the things you love to do.
I laid down naked in front of all of you,
Soulless, like a slave in disgusting view.
Every time you came, come, and cum
You ripped me into a thousand pieces.
And that's something all of you
Will never understand.
And that's something precious
You took in one glance.

WOMAN

I guess I will never understand.
The kind of woman, inside a woman.
Nor a thousand beautiful souls,
Living in one mysterious heart.
It's like having the moon and
the sun at the same moment in time.
A child, a girl, a woman, and a warrior
trapped in the labyrinth of her eyes.
I thought I knew it all,
I wish I could hold her smiles,
I wanted to, I need her so.
I was lost, as deeper and deeper I go.
Unpredictable. Gentle and yet, strong.
The kind of strength not shown,
Gracious and so powerful, but
Always has a loving heart.
You are a woman,
Bearer of light and darkness.
The goddesses of Venus.
Wise, brilliant, and sizzling sexy.

THE WIDOW

Hear the sobbing silence
The feeling of not seeing the one
Who's been there and often comes around
As the mourning woman stands still.
In pouring rain of this sacred ground
The silent eyes looking down
With hands shivering in lonely sound
Speechless and yet, trying to hold.
Upon the last memories of the man
That turns her life into gold
What mystery it will be
To go on living without him today?
The children are old and no longer play
Who will embrace her in the night
And say, darling I am here to stay.
Life in the fading colours of the wind
As the sand of the shore burrows her feet
She whispered in gentle words and said,
My love, you may not be here today
Remember my heart died
With you on that day.

BROKEN

I used to fly, not low and not that high
People see me as ordinary as I can be
My colours painted in blue, red and gray
The world seems nice so I go astray.
I met bees, buzzing my way
And eagles are cruel as they say
From flowers to roses I play
Trees and hilltops, I stayed.
Until a creature came along
Too wise and I guess too strong
Took me into his palm and said
I promise you the stars someday.
Amazed at how the dream is portrayed
I allowed myself to believe and be played
For eight long years indeed, I've waited
Until I saw myself drowning in misery.
I cried for promises unfulfilled
Looking up still hoping I could reach
So, I asked the creature why I was fooled
It replied and smiled, that's beyond this world.

TEARS IN THE DARK

For I am scared.
Never felt so afraid.
From the wolves,
Who roamed the earth.
For my hands are tied,
Neither my brave spirit
Is broken.
I am trapped inside these walls,
I am helpless to fight for all.
I am powerless to kill,
I am ill.
The sickness of worrying all the time.
The future which blinded by dark rhymes.
The tears of sadness and poetry,
Begins to beg and finally fall.
As I kneeled down,
In silent sound beyond words.
Like a murmuring monster
Who awaits to be freed,
Full of anguish and desperate
Vengeance, I shouted in agony.
But no one heard my voice.
And no one cares to listen.
All I've felt is my bleeding eyes,
And the blood that rolls upon my cheeks.
I am alone in the dark.

STONES IN THE WATER

I am nobody,
floating away in the water
it's calm and cold and
I hear nothing.
I am slowly drowning,
like a sunset up above me
fading away in the horizon and
no one even cares.
I am in pain,
each wound is sinking
like stones in the water and
my is heart is heavier every day.
I am hoping,
catching my breath.
I am dying,
without a worth.

THE CIRCUS OF LIFE

Welcome to the circus of life,
And see the freaks come alive.
The crowd of judgmental men
Laughing at your very worst pain.
Clown juggling in a thin wire,
Between the past, the present
And what else must still remain?
Smile, it pays to be mentally insane.
Hide your tears, act as if
Even if you bleed in his cruel game,
Of course, the sacrifice is for them.
The family, the children, and the dream.
You are the laughing clown
The one crucified by this town.
No matter how sad you frowned,
You always wear a laughing gown.

BEYOND THAT BRIDGE

I wish I knew where it mends,
A journey too long to end.
My heart is tired and weary,
Listening to everyone's story.
Every mile, I paused for a while.
Even if, it feels like an exile.
I tried to catch my breath,
And wonder how life does taste?
If I die today, love
remains a mystery.
A kind of myth, every man
dreams so sweet.
Beyond that bridge is a mist.
A fogging light that blinds my quest.
Whatever awaits in the edge,
Life is one hell of a blizz!

DREAM

I never saw you in a dream,

Quite beautiful as it seems.

A heart knows where it came

But I lost you in the end.

I awaken crying in the wind,

In the midst of all my pains.

A tale I hope will never end.

Somehow, I still do pretend.

Night after night you'd come again,

And all things mend in just,

In just one more, for a stunning dream.

ABOUT THE AUTHOR

Miss Diana D. Deocareza is a Master Teacher II of San Vicente Elementary School. She shows exemplary competence and outstanding performance. She is active in school activities, researches, innovative materials, projects, programs, and community services. She has a good moral character, good human relations in the school and the community, a model of morality and integrity both in my public and private life. She is kind, God-loving, honest, helpful, resourceful, has a strong work ethic, family-oriented, happy, and willing to offer service no matter what the task is. Her advocacy is to create an impact in the lives of children and the community. Her dedication towards teaching is being ignited by her passion to mold young people, a catalyst for change, and helps the people in the community to be more transparent, ethical, and accountable for the improvement of the schools' performance.

She is a writer. She writes worktext, lesson plan, teachers' module plan in Singapore Mathematics for grades 4 to 6 teachers, and poems.

She has been a sole author and an oral presenter at the International Research Congress on February 22-25,2019 at Corus Hotel Kuala Lumpur, Malaysia on Action Research entitled, "The Effects of Learning Styles on the Academic Performance in Mathematics of Grade Six Pupils in San Vicente Elementary School.

Currently, she is the Senior Member of the Royal Institution Singapore, an active member of Rotary International and Boy Scouts of the Philippines. She is also an active member and served as Lector and Commentator in Saint Clement Parish Church.

In addition, she is the District Mathematics Coordinator, District MTAP Coordinator, District test constructor and test consolidator in Mathematics, District MEA/SBM/ESIP Coordinator, and School Librarian. She provides technical assistance to teachers to improve their competencies, takes active participation in the planning and implementation of training programs in the school, district and division levels, initiates improvement in instructional programs, leads in the preparation of instructional materials. She conducts INSET and LAC Sessions of Teachers, mentors co-teachers in content and skill difficulties through observation of classes, and the Teacher Induction Program for beginning teachers.

She earned her Complete Academic Records in Doctor of Education from the University of Rizal System Morong, Rizal, and got a full scholarship from Governor Ynares. She earned her Master's Degree from Tomas Claudio Memorial College. She attended her undergraduate studies at the University of Rizal System Morong, Rizal and got a full scholarship from Coca Cola Foundation, and received an award for Most Outstanding Student Teacher.

In terms of major awards, in 2020 she received awards for National Excellence Award as Master Teacher and National Excellence Award in Research in LEAD Philippines.

In 2019, she received an award for Most Outstanding Elementary Teacher in Gawad Kampilan, Outstanding Public Elementary Teacher in Guronasyon, Outstanding Unit Leader in BSP given by AMUSCOM.

In 2018, she was one of the finalists in Guronasyon. She is a Senior Member of the Royal Institution Singapore, an active member, director, and chairman of the education and induction program

of Rotary International Rizal Urban Club and Boy Scouts of the Philippines.

9 786218 253773